Dear Shelby,

A wedding is a very special celebration and we are honored that you will be part of ours. We hope you are looking forward to it as much as we are. You will make a terrific flower girl!

Love,

Aunt Amy
&
Uncle John

Flower Girl

by **Barbara Bottner**   photographs by **Laura Grier**

Marshall Cavendish Children

Marshall Cavendish Corporation
99 White Plains Road
Tarrytown, NY 10591
www.marshallcavendish.us/kids

Library of Congress Cataloging-in-Publication Data
Bottner, Barbara.
Flower girl / by Barbara Bottner ; photographs by Laura Grier. – 1st ed.
p. cm.
Summary: A young girl prepares for and participates in the wedding of her favorite aunt.
ISBN 978-0-7614-6119-7 (hardcover) – ISBN 978-0-7614-6122-7 (ebook)
[1. Flower girls–Fiction. 2. Weddings–Fiction. 3. Aunts–Fiction.]
I. Grier, Laura, ill. II. Title.
PZ7.B6586Fl 2012   [E]–dc23   2011016394

Book design by Virginia Pope
Editor: Robin Benjamin

Printed in Malaysia (T)
First edition
10 9 8 7 6 5 4 3 2 1

For Miranda Nicole
–B.B.

I want to thank our little stars, Sydney and Robert, for working so hard to be
the best flower girl and ring bearer that I have had a chance to photograph.
I also want to thank Monika at the Trump National Golf Club for allowing
their gorgeous venue to be our backdrop for this story. Most importantly, I owe
a HUGE debt of gratitude to Mark, Monica, Rosie, Katie, and Alana for not
only planning this gorgeous wedding, but for donating their valuable time to the
completion of this book. I hope this book will be the first one on the shelves of
Mark and Monica's new nursery when their little one finally enters this world.
–L.G.

All my friends have been flower girls.

Violet was a flower girl.

Lillibelle was a flower girl.

Fiona was a flower girl, too.

Everybody has been a flower girl . . .

but me.

But today, my aunt Penny is getting married.

And guess who her flower girl is . . . ?

When you're a flower girl,
you get to wear flowers in your hair

and carry a bouquet and wear fancy shoes.

But the best part
is that I get to
wear a white dress
like Aunt Penny's.

This is Kevin—who will be my *uncle* Kevin
as soon as he marries my aunt Penny—and his
nephew Henry, who will be his ring bearer.
They're funny.

Aunt Penny and her bridesmaids are almost ready.
They don't look nervous, but I am.

Henry's a little nervous, too.

I give him a good luck kiss, but he says, "No thanks!"

It's time for the ceremony.
I take a deep breath.

The wedding music begins.
I walk down the aisle with Henry. Everyone watches.

This is Aunt Penny's
big moment. Here she comes
with her dad.

I get to stand in front
and watch the ceremony.

Uncle Kevin and Aunt Penny are married now!

"You did a great job," my aunt Penny tells me.

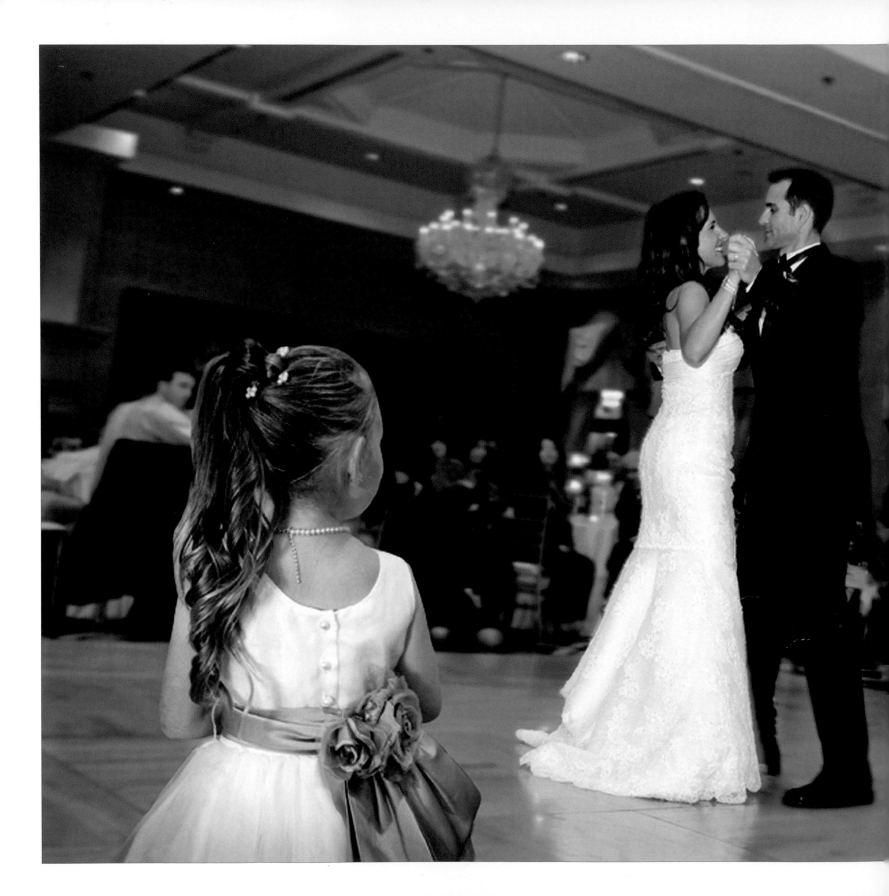

It's time for the party!
Aunt Penny and Uncle Kevin
have the first dance.

Then we ALL dance.

It's the best night ever.

And then there's cake!

I wish I could go to a wedding every day.

One day maybe I'll be a bride. I'll be as happy as Aunt Penny.

And at my wedding, there will be a flower girl, too.